The Rainbow of the Dream

FIRST EDITION

©opyright 2016 by Gary Drury Publishing™

ISBN-10: 0692699805
ISBN-13: 978-0692699805 (Gary Drury Publishing)

DrurysPublishing.com

Kentucky

Produced in The United States of America.

Contents

Poems

PET HEAVEN

There's a place beyond the rainbow
That God prepared with care
So when our pets must leave us
We'll know that they are there.

It is a special sanctum
Where they can rest and play,
Knowing we will claim them
Again some joyous day.

Our bond will be renewed
Just as it was before;
The undying love of a pet —
You cannot ask for more.

I pray for such a Heaven,
For in my heart I know
Wherever He does take them—
That's where I want to go.

— © C. David Hay

SILENT TWILIGHT

I miss the call of the whip-poor-will
That echoed through the wood,
And lament the barren stumps
Where majestic trees once stood.

Hush too, the mystic shadow bird
Who hooted away the night,
Then retreated to his vanished den
Before dawn's glowing tight.

The symphonies of twilight time
Were solace to the soul —
Wise men know to leave untouched
What's best in God's control.

How sad the loss of that we love;
Too late we fail to see —
The treasures of the moment
Someday may cease to be.

— © C. David Hay

A GRAIN OF SAND

Who am I that GOD should hear
The prayers I utter through the year?
I am but a grain of sand,
But still a part of what HE,S planned.
HE counts each grain and knows that we
Together, make a mighty sea
Of people, who rever HIS ways
And raise our voices filled with praise,
For who HE is and what HE'S done.
For love so great HE gave HIS son,
That we may all receive the choice
To walk with HIM, and hear HIS voice.

— © **Betty Lou Hebert**

RED SUNSET

Clouds rise like foam, behind the dome
Of mountains in the west.
The sun shoots sprays of golden rays
That pierce the clouds soft breast,
And from inside, a blood-red tide
Of color soon appears
And flushes all the vaporous wall,
As darkness slowly nears.
Then when the light gives way to night,
The western sky still shows,
For many miles, in crimson piles,
Clouds tinted like a rose!

— © **Betty Lou Hebert**

A PRECIOUS DAY

The ancient hills in beauty stand
Above this vast and lonely land,
Against a sky of flawless blue,
A soaring eagle scans the view.
The sign of man, a dusty trail,
Winding through the sage and shale.
No sound of man assaults the air.
Only silence everywhere.
Down from the heights on a wintry day,
The frost god flings his jewels away.
Diamonds, lying on the snow,
In icy splendor, beauty show.
Up from the desert, flushed with light,
A thousand wings flash, silver bright,
As small birds rise in disarray,
To greet another precious day!

— © Betty Lou Hebert

TRUE LOVE

One day she was there
the next she was gone;
With no word of goodbye
she left me alone.
The fault was all mine
such sorrow I now bear—
I ignored her impassioned pleas
without thought or care;
She loved me as no other
but the truth I never knew
And thus I broke her heart
and lost a love forever true.

— © Herbert Jerry Baker

WHAT IS IT?

What is it that we do the best?
That reminds us of those
Days now past, and
Of the days to come?
We blow up things,
Our fireworks we welcome
A new year and we holler and sing
And in our big show
We celebrate our wars,
Our fire bursting into star glow!
We sing of our capacity for war.
Man's sin is showing.
But God sees our awful ways:
Turning from Him to direct our own course.
But He forgives and directs us still!
Oh Blessed Lord, our Kinsman Redeemer!
Our shout of praise rises to You.
Direct our Peace, and in just wars.
May our praise be louder and more sincere
Than all the bombs we drop in fear!

— © Ken Gillespie

SOFT WHISPERS II

By The Bend In
The Mighty Wolf River
— © Ken Gillespie

There was an owl who who lived in the woods,
In the deep, dark woods by the trail,
And late at night he came out to sing
Many songs, my ancestors tell.

And he sang of the woods and the flowers there
By the trail that crossed the stream
At Estaunaulla where the river bends
And the big Oak long ago fell.

And he sang of the gold that was buried there
Neath the Oak by the curve of the river
Near the town that was there til the yankees came
And burned it. now' no one can tell

Where the town stood then by the bank of the river
By the curve where the big Oak fell,
The owl still sings his lonely song
In the deep, dark words by the trail.

"Come, here's the gold" and the diggers run
Digging holes in the flowering dell;
"No! It's over here, no it's over there"
And they run and they run pell-mell.

How many have perished? No one can tell,
But the owl keeps count and sings his song,
"Come to Estaunaulla and find my gold."
But some they say think the devil's there.

And for gold they just dig into hell!
But they keep a cornin'
The devil's song hummin'
And the owl laughs beside his trail.

— © Ken Gillespie

DAVE'S READY

the new clothes
are ready
and laid out

the little rag rug
is bought

he has all of the supplies
on the list

crayons
thick pencil #2
A Big Chief
rounded scissors
and glue
all sacked up
to go

it's all there

he's met the teacher
and she's pretty
he's seen his room
they have hamsters
and guppies

it will be fun
he knows

now if I
can just let him

go

— © **Sheryl L. Nelms**

LOVERS WALK THE BEACH

Pristine sand kissed by the waves
shines with a brilliant light
sent down from a shiny sun
so golden and so bright.

Sea Gulls dance upon the waves
and ride the gentle tides
looking for a bite to eat
enjoying nature's ride.

On this torrid summer day
as gulls fly in the air
two young lovers holding hands
speak of the life they'll share.

So, on this day of sharing love
they walk upon the sand
vowing they will always stay
as they hold each others hand.

— © **Sheila B. Roark**

TOGETHER AGAIN

The sisters used to be so close
growing and learning each day,
but when they grew up they decided
to live their lives far, far away.

They were too busy to visit their father
the man who chased all of their fears,
the man who loved them with all of his heart
and spent time wiping their tears.

When the Cancer was found by the doctors
attacking him both day and night
his daughters came back to be with him
to help him be strong and to fight.

Once again they were gathered together
supporting their weak and sick dad
talking about the times that they shared
and all of the love that they had.

So, as they watch him get sicker
and fade from their wet, heavy eyes,
they lean on each other to keep going
as they mourn their sweet father's demise.

The girls quietly wait by his bedside
praying that he will not die,
but knowing the time is approaching
when he'll say his final goodbye.

— © **Sheila B. Roark**

KEEPER OF THE PAST

I still plant new flowers every spring
And wait for colored promises they bring.
I search to find the first star of the night
And make a wish upon it's twinkling light.
Although I know that nothing stays the same,
Still, I won't let the wind forget your name.
I'll keep alive the lovely songs we sang,
Remembering the way our voices rang.
And I will act in days still left tome,
As keeper of the way things used to be.

— © **Betty Lou Hebert**

A MAN FROM DAKOTA

Within the precinct house there sat
A homeless man with battered hat.
His eyes were gazing at the past.
The sorrow in his features cast
A shaft of sympathy for one
Who felt his life was nearly done.

His name was Bill and he had come
From North Dakota. That's the sum
Of knowledge he supplied and yet,
Somehow we never could forget
The haunted eyes, the hopeless air,
That emanated from him there.

An officer, with camera came
And verified this transient's name.
Then took a picture, capturing,
The essence of Bill's wandering
And when enlarged, it had appeal.
Emotions shown were so real.

It hung awhile up on display
And everyone who passed that way,
Was taken by the quality.
The great despair that all could see.
But now, it hangs upon our wall.
A homeless man, home, after all!

— © **Betty Lou Hebert**

FRESH MEMORIES

I remember days upon the dunes,
Where the ocean sang us salty tunes!
We hiked and sat to stare at all the sand
And hold the warmth of it within a hand.
It sifted through our fingers just like time.
We weren't aware, for being in our prime,
But now in looking back I wonder why
We didn't know that life was passing by!
How different our days then might have been
If for a single moment we had seen
How brief those carefree hours on the shore.
How many years would pass again before
I'd find myself in that same place and see
That being there alone was misery!
Yet I still cling to memories that stay
As fresh as though they took place yesterday!

— © **Betty Lou Hebert**

I SAW MY NAME IN THE SKY

I had a vision in my
mind's eye as I gazed
into that expanse of azure
blue and through imagination
the machination of a dream
came to delight my soul.
I saw my name in the sky
proclaiming that one-day I
would know success
is coming to greet me
and keep me in its palm
to soothe me like a psalm
singing lullaby to calm
my impatient spirit.
I felt its warmth like
a blanket, a full belly
at a lavish banquet
to appease and please
my hungry heart that
threatened to depart
my faith and hope.
Life was a broken remote
that smote my TV screen
blank and black
never coming back
with movie portraying
my dream fulfilled.
My name in the sky
tells me I will not
be a failure 'till I die;
the sky is my blackboard
and destiny signed it!

— © **Gerald Heyder**

SEDGWICK COUNTY JUVENILE OFFICER
In memory of my father

He always worried about his kids

the runaways who traveled hell
before he found them
the beaten children

the two-year-old he talked about
for days wondered how
a mother could do that
to her own baby

the neglected kids

he cried once for the eight kids
he found living in a miniature house
with seven dogs and rooms full of flies
and dog shit and a bottle of Ketchup

the sexually used kids

men who did that to children
made him mad enough to kill
he said very slowly

in the kids he had hope
always said there was no
such thing as a bad kid

he gave them his best
until he got ulcers and a nervous break down
but his kids always came first

— © **Sheryl L. Nelms**

LIGHT

Born unto hands of fate
Whether soon or late
Each man must perish
Greet his grim reaper
Implore favorable destination
A noble honorable just soul
Holds kiting glory
A nefarious rogue harden soul
Warriors for peace eternally
Righteousness harbors
Neutral ground
Leveling consequences
Equally and justifiably
Where faith resides
Lovingly in engrossing heart
Each man must harness
Strength despite tribulations,
Overcome inconceivable odds
Light shall pierce darkness
Blazing path to true freedom
Whether soon or late
Each man must perish
Discovering his darkness,
Discovering his Light.

— © **Gary Drury**

SECRET PLACE

She keeps her private thoughts
in a place only she knows,
found in the deep recesses of her mind
safely hidden from those around her.

Only God is allowed in her secret place
and when she invites Him in
He blesses her with needed peace
and the strength to carry on.

It is here she can speak to God
knowing He will understand
and always ease the pain she feels
as she struggles through her life.

She reserves this place for her sweet Lord
speaking to Him through prayer,
and in return He smiles upon her
gracing her with His deep and lasting love.

— © **Sheila B. Roark**

HERE COMES THE SNOW

The little house stands all alone
surrounded by tall trees
welcoming flakes of falling snow
as they dance upon the breeze.

The icy snow falls gracefully
from gray clouds in the sky,
and covers trees with ermine coats
as hushed as a lullaby.

It also falls upon the house
which shines with crystal light
created by the falling snow
that floats throughout the night.

All is hushed this winter night
now muted by the snow
that gently falls from clouds above
and shines with spirit glow.

— © **Sheila B. Roark**

ANOTHER YEAR

Another year goes limping by
injured by disaster and war,
heavy from heartache men cannot hide
as they ask what the battles are for?

All people pray as they go through each day
that mankind will finally find peace,
wanting to live in a world full of joy
where sadness and all problems cease.

But the battles keep raging around us
destroying the world that we know
leaving destruction behind them
along with a deeply felt woe.

Maybe next year will be better,
a time when we find blessed peace
and live out our lives with contentment
where sadness and all problems cease.

— © Sheila B. Roark

THE ELOQUENT EYES

Who is able to translate the passion better,
Than ardent, bright, eloquent eyes,
Who sends you an enigmatic letter,
Who invites you to soar in the sky?
Who tell you something you cannot hear,
Initiate the secret sighs,
Who once now love, now burst into tears?
You, my beloved eloquent eyes!

— © **Adolf P. Shvedchikov, PhD, LittD**
International Poet of Merit

MY FANTASIES ARE ENDLESS, YES!

My fantasies are endless, yes!
Don't worry, let my fancy roam,
I have opened doors in my home,
Let them walk wearing a queer dress.
I like the quirks, nevertheless,
Uncover the cage of your mind,
Give me a chance to remind
That mad ideas make progress!

— © **Adolf P. Shvedchikov, PhD, LittD**
International Poet of Merit

THE WORLD WILL BE SAVED
BY BEAUTY AND ART

In this cruel life where coexists
Heavenly love and dreadful death,
I believe in the beauty's eternal fiesta
To the rest of life, to my last breath!
I don't know how long the terror will rule,
How often new bloody wars will start?
To survive, we must use a reliable tool:
The world will be saved by beauty and art!

— © **Adolf P. Shvedchikov, PhD, LittD**
International Poet of Merit

THE WIND DOESN'T BLOW

The wind doesn't blow, all my sails
Have weighed down in the motionless air.
There is long calm, a time of despair,
I think, alas, that all past life fails.
And a vagrant thoughts whisper again
About balance between death and life,
Between sweet peace and bloody strife,
About roses which will wane.
But it doesn't help to suppress my pain,
I cannot transform black into white.
It seems Ecclesiastes was right
To say: everything was in vain!

— © **Adolf P. Shvedchikov, PhD, LittD**
International Poet of Merit

KANSAS COMFORT

nothing is
more soothing

than
the barbed

rustle

of fields
full

of tan wheat

waiting
to be

cut

— © **Sheryl L. Nelms**

IN GRAM'S GARDEN

the back porch is shaded
by white lattice frothed

with pink roses

under the steps
a mossed corner

is full of the delectable sweetness
of lily-of-the-valley

behind the detached garage
stands a long row

of red hollyhocks

along the east side
of the house marches

the royal purple

of iris

and out
in the garden
under the clothesline

blooms three rows of
orange zinnias

covered with
the thick flutter

of yellow butterflies

— © Sheryl L. Nelms

GALVESTON'S EBB AND FLOW

coming
and going

seashells
seaweed

sand smoothed froth

loll of
jelly fish

gull
tracks

turtle
eggs

leaves me
looking

under
rocks

— © Sheryl L. Nelms

BLACK HILLS SPRING

wind rustled

the churn
of meadow grass

hides frogs

strings croaks
 out of

every
green stalk

— © **Sheryl L. Nelms**

BUTTERFLY IN FLIGHT

a monarch
dips

thru the space

between
two

spruce trees

lifts up
and power

dives across
bluegrass

then flip
flip

flips its wings
into an

orange Double Flyer

windsurfing
over

the housetop

— © Sheryl L. Nelms

A MISTY DAY

The air is heavy with moisture
creating a soggy blanket
that slowly covers sleeping trees
with an eerie coating of wetness.

Bare limbs can be seen
piercing the heavy fog,
with twisted, arthritic fingers
reaching out from the charcoal mist.

The misty day is tinted gray
and as the fog moves on,
the trees seem to disappear
under a coating of wet grayness.

All is quiet on this day
silenced by the heavy fog
that blankets the sleeping trees
as they dream of the coming spring.

— © **Sheila B. Roark**

WHERE ARE THEY?

It is a hushed and eerie night
as one lone schooner quietly glides
cutting through the lapping waves
of the dancing, dark, and rhythmic tides.

There is no movement on the ship,
no sounds are heard this night,
for her crew has disappeared
though no on knows their plight.

On and on the lone boat sails
with no real place to go,
propelled by the spirit of the sea
it rides the water's flow.

What happened to the crew this night?
We may never know
if they are floating in the sea
awash with spirit glow?

So, on this night the boat glides on
no men or crew in sight,
an empty ship upon the sea
that sails throughout the night.

— © Sheila B. Roark

UNDER THE MOONLIGHT

The day has now retired
replaced by the dark of night
lit brightly by a silver, glowing moon
shining down on the serene lake.

The only sounds heard this night
are the steady drone of cicadas,
and the gentle lapping of the water
as it caresses the sides of a lone rowboat.

The couple are enjoying the night
so happy to be together,
enjoying the time they are sharing
lost in a world of their own.

The silver rays shine down on them
lighting them with a diamond beacon
as brilliant as the love they share
on this calm and quiet night.

They stay on the lake for hours,
enjoying the peace of the night
and the completeness they both feel
just sharing each others company.

When it is time to leave
they softly kiss goodbye
and promise to meet again
for they need each other to survive.

— © **Sheila B. Roark**

SURROUNDED BY DARK CLOUDS

Her loneliness attacks her daily
piercing her heart with deep misery
as she numbly goes through her days
under a blanket of dark clouds.

She has no one in her life to love her
no one she can talk to
or share her hopes and dreams,
creating a gaping hole of emptiness in her being.

Her sadness completely envelopes her
blocking out all happiness and joy,
bringing on unending tears
as she lays in her bed at night alone.

Her fondest wish is to find love
to make her feel whole again,
but for now all she has is misery
and the dark clouds that won't go away.

— © **Sheila B. Roark**

AT MIDNIGHT

The town clock has just chimed midnight,
and by the docks all is quiet
except for the rhythmic sloshing of the water
gently caressing the moored boats.

A blanket of misty fog has moved in
slowly coiling around the boats
swallowing their masts
like a hungry animal after a kill.

The glow from the street lights
eerily shines through the thick fog
creating strange shadows on the deserted streets
on this damp and silent night.

It seems as if all life has been drained
from this part of town
which slumbers peacefully
under a blanket of the foggy mist.

— © **Sheila B. Roark**

Stories

SNOW STORM IN THE KITCHEN

© by Sheila B. Roark

Having twins filled my life with pastel rainbows and the golden rays of happiness. Now that they are grown with children of their own, I fondly look back at the time when they were growing up and smile remembering some of their crazy antics. There was never a dull moment during those early years and one day in particular comes to mind that I shall never forget, it was the day we had a major snow storm in the kitchen.

The "storm" occurred on a bright, sunny spring day filled with the joy of rebirth. Trees were budding and animals scampered here and there preparing for the babies that would arrive soon. That day my girls were in a very playful mood. I have to keep a close eye on them, I thought, they look like they're up to no good.

At the age of two and a half, the girls were extremely active and very curious about everything. Exploring was one of their favorite things to do. They loved to open closets to see what they could find. So, when I left them in the kitchen for a few moments alone, they set out on one of their adventures.

After opening two of the closet doors they could reach, Meri found the Tide and Teri found the potato chips and flour. Then the fun began! Meri dumped the entire box of Tide on the floor. Not to be outdone, Teri emptied the bags of potato chips and flour on top of the Tide! Then they preceded to mix everything together, lay on it, and throw it all over the kitchen and each other!

When I returned I couldn't believe my eyes. The kitchen I had just cleaned was coated with a film of snowy white and an occasional potato chip was stuck here and there. The girls were covered in white from head to toe!

It looked like a blizzard had hit the kitchen! They were having such a wonderful time playing snow storm they didn't hear me when I returned.

There was Tide and flour covering the floor, the counters, the cabinets, the sink, the kitchen table, the kitchen carpet, and of course, all over the girls. They looked like little snowmen with hazel eyes.

I just stood there with my mouth opened not able to say a word. After the shock wore off, I laughed until I cried. I hugged them both and gave them a much needed bath and put them in their playpen so they couldn't get into any more trouble, at least for a while. It took me a long time to clean up the "storm" and by the time I was finished the girls had fallen asleep.

After a lot of hard work everything looked clean again, that is, except the rug. I couldn't get all the "snow" out of it and years later there were still reminders of the day we had a snow storm in our kitchen on a warm spring day.

Yes, they were always quite a handful usually going in different directions and driving me crazy, but I wouldn't have traded them for the world. We learned a lot from each other during those years of trial and error and today they are two of the best friends I have. Even though they are now adults, they still find ways to fill my heart with rainbows by sharing their precious friendship and love with me.

I'LL NEVER FORGET HER

© by Sheila B. Roark

It has been a long time since I have been in the eighth grade, but after almost a lifetime of living, I still remember my favorite teacher from elementary school. She was a unique character, to say the least, and one I shall never forget.

I attended Notre Dame School for twelve years. It was a private girl's school in midtown Manhattan run by a group of very caring and loving nuns. In those days, they wore a full habit which always demanded respect from all the girls who were part of the Notre Dame family. Their flowing black gowns, and heart shaped head pieces emphasized their deep devotion to their calling. Everyone who attended their school loved them dearly, including me. Since they were our surrogate mothers during the day, we called them Mother. The practice in other Catholic schools was to call the nuns Sister, but not at Notre Dame, our nuns wanted their school to be our home away from home, and to have the nuns become our second mothers.

Notre Dame is a college preparatory school which emphasized learning and has very few extra curriculum activities. I had many good teachers during my twelve years at Notre Dame, which has now become a high school, but my favorite teacher was Mother Genevieve.

She was only five feet tall and about six feet wide, with eyes the color of a new spring morning that always shined with an impish twinkle. Her face was as fair and fine as alabaster, and her smile lit up the room. When she got mad, it never lasted long, and in a short time she would bounce back to her usual cheery self.

She was more than just a teacher, she was an entertainer who would perform in the strangest ways to emphasize our lessons. I remember one day in an eighth grade drama class she was teaching us how to do a death scene properly. The next thing I knew, she was laying on the floor with her feet in the air. Of course, the class was stunned not knowing what to do. We just stood there with our mouths opened afraid to move. She laid on the floor for about thirty seconds, arose with the dignity of a queen, and as she smoothed out her habit declared, "Now girls, that's how you do a dying scene."

Then there were the days when we would get her annoyed. When Mother Genevieve got mad at us for not paying attention, she would do strange things with her eyes. She would move them back and forth with such speed, we thought they would take flight. Her soft blue eyes became a blur as she scanned the room searching for trouble makers. Of course this always stopped any noise immediately and enabled her to continue her lesson of the day.

When she wasn't demonstrating dying scenes, or moving her eyes at mach speed, she was a wonderful teacher. She was able to make our lessons come alive in a way no other teacher could. When she taught us about the middle ages, we could feel the coldness of the castles where kings lived, and the pain the serfs suffered as they toiled in the fields.

When we studied about China, she taught us Chinese writing and let us sample some of the food the people eat. She opened up the

Asian world to us and helped us understand what it is like to live there.

She also taught us to love our language and to appreciate it's beauty by analyzing the works of the masters in her own unique way. She would have us read these works out loud so we could savor their magnificence which made these masterpieces come alive for us. She always made her lessons so vibrant that we looked forward to going to school each day. No one ever wanted to miss anything Mother Genevieve had to say.

She had other wonderful qualities beside being a gifted teacher. She was always available to listen and advise if anyone needed a strong shoulder to lean on. She never turned anyone away who needed her help in any way, and tried to be a friend to all.

This woman, who was loved by all, was a combination of a comic, a teddy bear, and a brilliant teacher. She magically opened up the world to me enabling me to appreciate its wonder and beauty. I recently heard that she passed away and feel a tremendous sense of loss over her passing. I often think of her and of all the precious gifts she gave me so long ago. My hope is that every child who attends school is lucky enough to have a teacher like Mother Genevieve so that they too can think back to their school days with fond memories like me.

GRANDPA JOHN AND MAMAW MARY'S HOUSE UP GABE ROAD PAST CLENDENIN, WV.

© by Juliet R. Lynch

The story goes that Grandpa John and Maw Mary were able to marry after he got in touch with her and asked if she would marry him. She said YES, but they didn't meet until the day they married.

Grandpa Foreman was 6 feet tall and 175 lbs , barrel chested man and very strong for his size and worked from day light to dark six days a week and Sunday was his day of rest. Grandpa, paid $2,500.00 for 800-acre farm and found Deed and it was NO GOOD. Had to pay for it second time.

Their house was made of rough sawed lumber with a tin roof. Inside the kitchen was a wood burning stove with side water chambers. On Saturday night the water chambers were filled with water several times so that the wash tub in the kitchen could be filled for baths. Saturday, the day was time for getting ready for Sunday Church and Sunday dinner and a day of rest on SUNDAY, before the farm work week and chores and school, for the kids on Monday. The Saturday started with the gathering of what was needed, to make the Lye soap and getting drinking water and making and storing pies and cakes for the week to come. The pie safe often held 10 to 15 pies and cakes. Some rested on the window sill in early spring and summer, covered with cheese cloth.

Maw always wore her apron and sometimes a Dust cap. She was about 5 feet 10 inches tall, and she began her work as home -keeper, baby watcher and meal fixer, along with mending and quilt making, and nursing the sick and afflicted. "So much to do and so little time to do it in." Paw seemed to cherish the wee morning hours as he lit the gas lights and built the fire in the stove, so Maw could begin the morning cooking with the aromas of ham and eggs and roasted coffee (chickoree) beans "for strong work coffee as the men called it." Biscuits, fried potatoes, gravy and fruit was either dehydrated or fresh.

One day, an Oxen dragged a sawed log over Grandpa Foreman, he put a wood splint on it and wrapped it in an old sheet, and went back to work. Grandpa Foreman, ran the Saw Mill , Grist Mill, and General Store.

The Family Tree of Foreman's

Harley Foreman, Nona Foreman, Anna Foreman, Oxeys Forman, Homer Foreman, Earnest Foreman, Genive Foreman.

The rooms of the house all had raised hearth fireplaces, handmade straight back chairs in the room and a chair beside the bed. A wash stand and basin to do cleansing and pitcher with water for rinsing. A WHITE Sewing Machine for in the corner (off limits to Children).

Living room had two full beds for guests and straw ticks and homemade quilts and feather pillows. There were Gas wall lights and two straight back home made chairs and a night stand for family the Family Bible.

Dining room had a rough sawed Oak Boards, two benches on each side of the table and one chair at each end for Pa and Ma. Table was set Country Style with food and after meal the table was covered up with a table cloth. There was no refrigerator!!!! If hungry you got a clean plate and uncover left over food. The Pie safe would have 10 to 12 Berry or Fruit pies. Gas wall lights and candles on table.

WHAT HAS CHANGED IN YOUR LIFE AND WHAT WILL YOU DO WITH IT

© by Juliet Rhodes Lynch

Today is a new day and you can make the best of every moment of it, or you can totally make a mess of it. I can watch in the directness of each day and wonder if we have lost the perspective of all that is precious and good in life. We can see the daily click of the clock, and watch the time fly by, then not realizing just how much time is wasted do to petty little things. You intend to do the laundry, write and pay the bills and get them mailed, run the sweeper, and clean out messy areas of the house that are filled with "stuff," that really needs to go to the trash and out the door. There is a list waiting to go to the grocery store, even one for mall shopping or the badly needed trip to area hardware or the bigger trip to Lowe's or Home Depot. The oft times last two trips will include the other part of past wasted time, when painting rooms in the house, or repairing certain things that you have let go. What about the extra electric plugs needed on the Sun Porch, the slight wiring of a small compact freezer you bought to have extra food, for times of 18 to 20 inches of snow no one seems to expect.

Each day filled with changes not always planned, nor are the changes what we have wanted, or did we continue on the directions which came with the changes or plans. Why can't we seem to move forward and onward to the better directions that would help us to make life a more viable better direction? Spend time of experiencing life, and what good things it can bring.

I project my mind to do certain things and even before I get out of bed in the morning I have ideas, on my mind that I really need to tackle for the day and maybe even for the next few days. I am a writer; a painter, crafter and I also have laundry to do and things to get at the neighborhood Dollar Store. Plenty of cleaning, even household chores that need to be done. They don't always get done. I wish I could wave a magic wand to cause all the mind changing ideas of what I want to be, and to get done, before I take my last breath in life.

One never knows if or when they will take their last breath!!! Does this make it of immediate importance of situations, that one should make changes in their lives? What are the changes that have come into my life and what changes do I want? I have found a faith that has grown stronger in me. I have knowledge of miracles that have happened and prayers that have been answered. I have close friends and family that care about me and even though my health isn't what I want it to be, I see the kindness in people who are helping me to deal with humor, the less than delightful walking and climbing situation of my legs and feet. The church we attend has a ramp for people to use that can't climb steps. On Sunday there is a man at our church that stands at the top of the ramp and waits for me to hand him the handle end of my cane and he helps me walk up the ramp. There is a group of family and church people who stand at the edge of the ramp to make sure I don't slide or need assistance. This goes on both going to church and when it's over. Now here is the humor to this, as I am climbing up the ramp or coming down, with all the assistance. There are cars going rapidly by on Route 4. It slows down and people are looking at me climbing the ramp. In their mind they are saying '' how many people does it take to get the ole lady up that ramp"? Usually the traffic goes fast on that road but during the ramp walk and me, it slows down. Lol

56

I see the world changing and right now not for the better. I see people who are being drawn away from the Lord and seem to have less happiness in their lives. The families' are drawn apart by addictive lives, such as television, cell phones, computers, drinking, drugs, abuse, divorce, robberies, and killings and soliciting. What else has come to our life, and brings terror to us, shootings, wars, and diseases.

you realize that all these things in our lives do not mean a thing as long as we don't have the Lord Jesus Christ in our lives? Your saying,'' well that's your business and not mine. I am not into religion or going to church." The TRUTH IS, THAT YOU MAY NEVER FIND PEACE AND YOU MAY NEVER KNOW HEAVEN IN YOUR LIFE. "WHO ARE YOU TO SAY THIS? YOU ARE NOT TO JUDGE ME".!!! I'm not judging you but I have come to the realization that in my own life there is a void when there is "STUFF". There needs to be guidance as there was in our parents and grandparents times. That, was what kept us in many areas of our lives. That was the right ways and the wrong ways of doing most everything. In most homes, God and the Bible were in the spirit of how we lived and in the roll of how we acted, and in what we believed in, that was RIGHT AND WHAT WAS WRONG. God ruled, AND was and always should be first in our lives. The father was most generally the head of the household. God is REAL and so is the DEVIL. The President and his ruling parties were backed by God, in their selection of what was to come then, now and in the future. Then, came PRAYERS OUT OF SCHOOL, THE FLAG WAS NOT PLEDGED TO, RULES CHANGED. MASSIVE terror, in Foreign Countries. Governments trying to take over every aspect of our lives. PEOPLE TURNING AGAINST EACH OTHER OVER RELIGION, greed for wanting what will set them free from their own countries, dictators and non- freedom.

We have lost our way and allow ourselves to be prisoners of greed, hate and destruction. We NEED TO CHANGE AND WE CAN IF WE ALLOW GOD BACK INTO OUR LIVES ON A MINUTE TO MINUTE BASIS.

Change is good, but we have to want IT and God, more than we want the sad fakeness of lives filled with all the bad things, that don't matter when you really look at the core of these things that are ''stuff.''

What can we do if we change, how can we make our lives better? We must give the Lord our repentance and ask Him to come into our lives. The commitment of this time making it permanent and giving Him all of ourselves. We must pick up our Bibles and read them and study them. THERE ARE ANSWERS TO EVERYTHING THAT GOD HAS GIVEN TO YOU. GUIDANCE THAT WILL KEEP YOU ON THE RIGHT JOURNEY. The prayers that come down to the very depth of life and just sit down, kneel down and have the daily "little talk with Jesus". That's what makes changes and life changes work. A NEW YEAR and a NEW LIFE, and CHANGES THE HAVE AND WILL MAKE A DIFFERENCE IF YOU CHOOSE AND WILL LET IT.

Biographies

Born 6/21/41. Parents Eda and William Forcellon. Spouse: Harry W. Barto. Children: William M. Barto. Education: Katherine Gibbs School, Union College, New Jersey, Seton Hall, New Jersey. Extensive travel: Egypt, France, Italy, and England. Occupation: Legal Secretary, Legislative Aide, Writer last 20 years. Memberships: Past President Friends of the Hunterdon Museum of Art, Director of Volunteers at the Hunterdon Museum of Art, New Providence Library Board, New Providence, New Jersey, Raritan Valley College Book Group. Honors: Golden Certificate Awards, Drury Publishing, Plaque of Appreciation from the New Providence Library Board, Listed in Who's Who in America 1999/2000 Who's Who in the East and 2000 Who's Who in America. Have been listed in numerous Who's Who's for all 68 the past years since 2000 including 2007. Personal note: Married for 41 years to husband, Harry, who died in 2001. One son, William, who died in 2000. I love to write. Writing defines who I am.

Publishing Credits: Thirteen stories published by Creative With Words, 2 stories published by Writer's Guidelines and News. One story published in Yesterday's Magazette, One story published in a Reminisce hard cover book "The Fabulous Fifties", 3 stories published in Reminisce Magazine, and two stories published in Good Old Days Magazine. Many stories in Drury anthologies and seven books of stories published by Drury Publishing.

Palm Sunday is a saga about an Italian American family growing up in Brooklyn. The story follows the adventures of this large warm family as they move from Brooklyn to New Jersey and some as far as Florida. However, no matter how far the family is flung from each other they gather each Palm Sunday and Christmas to celebrate the holiday and more importantly the family. The story centers on five female cousins and how they grow and prosper-their loves, joys and sorrows. The story moves between the present time and the past telling of their parents and grandparents and how the family came to this country. The story concerns the grandparents and parents and their lives and fortunes and the children who in turn grow to have children and even grandchildren of their own. Each Palm Sunday and Christmas the family members reconnect and join together sharing their lives.

born and raised in Pittsburgh, PA, lives there still with her husband of fifty-four years, Nick Mother, grandmother and great grandmother, now retired, spends much of her time reading and studying her Bible, working on her writing, which she has been involved in now for nineteen years. She writes poetry and short stories and loves the small press magazines from across the country which give her a chance to have her work published for which she is most grateful Having no formal education other than her GE.D. for a high school diploma, she believes whatever talent she may have has been given to her as a gift from her heavenly Father, to share her feelings which may in some way, be just what someone would like or need to hear. She hopes her writings express her passion for life, her love and devotion to God, family and country. All glory be to the LORD.

I'm widowed and live in the country, in north Idaho, with my handicapped son. We enjoy the life here and all the wildlife we see. I have two older offspring who are married.

I've been writing for many years, actually since I was around ten years old and have been writing steadily for the past fifteen years or so.

My interests are many and varied. I love to travel, read, write, do craft work, garden, cook, and enjoy music of many kinds.

Peggy Kennedy

has published over 600 poems, six stories, one short short story, and one essay. She is currently published in Gary Drury Publishing anthologies and the Drury Gazette and Inside Passages, the last published in Ketchikan, AK. where she currently resides.

She has been published for forty five years. She is currently working on a novel, Wolf's MOON. She practices green daily. She has been listed in WHO'S WHO IN POETRY for fifteen years.

Juliet R. Lynch

Flames of Mame
Juliet R. Lynch

Topics for my Poetry and Writings come from inspirational and personal life experiences. 2-Who's Who in Women's Executives 1989, 1990 World of Poetry . . . 2-Who's Who in Women's Executives 1991,1993. World of Poetry. 2 Golden Poet Trophy Awards 1989,1990. 4-Awards of Merit 1987, 1988, 1989, 1990. 2-2000 Noble American Woman 1991, 1992. 1-West Virginia State College Certificate of Merit. 2-American Poetry Association. 4-Awards Trophies for Poetical Achievement, 1989, 1990, 1994, 1996.

The American Poetry Association has printed some of her works in the following Anthology Treasure Books. American Poetry Anthology 1987 and 1990. Best New Poets 1989 and 1990. Loves Greatest Treasures 1988. The World of Poetry has printed some of her Poetry in the following Anthologies. Great Poems of the Western World. World of Poetry 1989 and 1990. World of Poetry 1989 and 1990. World Treasury of Golden Poems. Mrs Lynch has received listings in publications as follows: Anthology listing 2000 NOTABLE AMERICAN WOMEN. Who's Who World Wide Platinum 1992. Professional Societies, The American Biographical Association, The International Platform Association, 25 Year Member of the Charleston Woman's Club, 36 Year Member of the Clendenin Woman's Club, American Biographical Inner Circle, Who's Who World Wide Platinum 1993, West Virginia Writer's Inc., The National Library of Poetry, Golden Rod Conference of Writer's, Clendenin Public Library Board, Clendenin's Writer's Group. Publication by the Author: Joy In The Morning, Book of Written Poetry, Writings and Reading's for Community Affairs, Flames of Mame historical novel Drury's Publications . . . Anthologies and Publications of Poetry and Writings, The Clendenin Herald Newspaper and The Clendenin Town and Country Newspaper, The Country Times Newspaper, Certificate from Gary Drury Publisher Writer Laureate for Juliet Rhodes Lynch.

My goal since 1979 has been to have something in the mail every Friday. It works. I've had over 5,000 stories, articles and poems published in textbooks, anthologies and magazines. Fourteen collections of my poems have also been published. My poems have been used on TV, CD's, audio tapes for the blind, in Braille, on PBS radio and in mail art shows including a show in Osaka, Japan.

Adolf
P.
Shvedchikov

Russian scientist, poet and translator

Born May 11, 1937 in Shakhty, Russia. In 1960 he graduated from Moscow State University, Department of Chemistry. Ph.D. in Chemistry in 1967. Senior researcher at the Institute of Chemical Physics, Russian Academy of Sciences, Moscow. Since 1997 - the chief chemist of the company Pulsatron Technology Corporation, Los Angeles, California, USA. Doctor of Literature World Academy of Arts and Letters.

He published more than 150 scientific papers and about 600 of his poems indifferent International Magazines of poetry in Russia, USA, Brazil, India, China, Korea, Japan, Italy, Malta, Spain, France, Greece, England and Australia. He published also 17 books of poetry. His poems have been translated into Italian, Spanish, Portuguese, Greek, Chinese, Japanese, and Hindi languages.

He is the Member of International Society of Poets, World Congress of Poets, International Association of Writers and Artists, A. L. I. A. S. (Associazione Letteraria Italo-Australiana Scrittori, Melbourne, Australia). Adolf P. Shvedchikov is known also for his translation of English poetry ("150 English Sonnets of XVI-XIX Centuries". Moscow. 1992. "William Shakespeare. Sonnets." Moscow. 1996) as well as translation of many modern poets from Brazil, India, Italy, Greece, USA, England, China and Japan.

In 2013 he was nominated for the Nobel Prize for Literature.

I have lived in Columbus since 1988, and I am an Ohio native. I started writing poetry in 1994. My other hobbies include camping, biking, reading, and photography, to name a few. I have an associate degree in electronics from Columbus State Community College. I currently work for an electrician's shop on the north side of Columbus. We design and build circuit boards from the ground up.

Marian H. Youngquist

was born and raised in Salem, Oregon. Throughout her ninety years she has written for newspapers, magazines and won prizes for plays and poetry. After three novels—*Procula, The Rocky Road Year, A String of Pearls*, and a memoir (private), she is at work on a fourth novel. She also lectures on Roman history. She and her husband Ted, a retired Lutheran minister, live in Wauwatosa, WI. They have four children, six grandchildren, and four great granddaughters.

Born: September 24, 1927, Archer, Florida, lived also, total of 30 years in Kansas City, Kansas; Chattanooga, Tennessee; Louisville, Kentucky, and Detroit, Michigan. It was in Louisville when I began writing songs and poetry around 1977, Basically writing of my life. I have lived every one of them. They are about people who have touched my life in a special way, nature, my pets, love, spiritual. God has been my soul teacher and mentor. Numerous awards. I leave my works to bear witness to Christ Jesus. **Parents:** Zofia and John Gocek. **Spouse:** Charles R. Walden. **Children:** Lisa Maria Walden.

Index

www.druryspublishing.com

www.ingramcontent.com/pod-product-compliance
Lightning Source LLC
Chambersburg PA
CBHW070351130626

46556CB00007B/3128